GHOSTS AND LEGENDS OF FREDERICK COUNTY

TIMOTHY L. CANNON
AND
NANCY F. WHITMORE

ILLUSTRATED BY DARBY PANNIER

PRINTED BY: STUDIO 20, INC., FREDERICK, MARYLAND

GHOSTS
AND
LEGENDS
OF
FREDERICK COUNTY

Contents

To Barbara

INTRODUCTION

In the late summer of 1976, we—the authors—inspired by the recent publication of Steve Brown's book *Haunted Houses of Harpers Ferry*, decided it might be fun to write a similar book about Frederick County. As we knew of some haunted houses and had access to other material, we eagerly got started. What we thought would be a three-month project quickly expanded into almost three years of interviews, research, and traversing the county many times.

The material we gathered seemed to fall into five areas. Hence, the book is divided into five parts or sections.

The first part is devoted solely to genuine haunted houses of Frederick County. Most of the material was gathered by conducting extensive interviews with people who lived in or came in contact with these houses. The incidents depicted here can be attested to by at least one living person and usually more.

The other four parts are based on material in local interest books and newspaper articles. All the material in these sections depicts events or tells stories that have some connection with the supernatural.

The first chapter in each of the five parts consists of some introductory words for that section followed by material we felt could not stand alone in a chapter by itself. The other chapters in each part deal with one subject.

To our families—especially Nancy, Mark and Chris—we wish to express our gratitude for their patience and understanding.

We would also like to thank the following: the staff of the Middletown *Valley Register,* former *News Post* reporters George May and Nick Wood, Mrs. Anne Selckmann, Steve Brown, Mrs. Nora Shepley, and Tim Baldwin.

Special thanks to our printer and friend Paul Farley of Studio 20, and Barbara Scott, for whom this book is dedicated.

HAUNTED

HOUSES

Local Haunts

Many great men have believed in the existence of ghosts or discarnate entities. It is said that Presidents Franklin D. Roosevelt and Harry Truman believed in ghosts and that Abraham Lincoln participated in seances when he was in the White House. The writer and humorist Mark Twain also participated in seances in hopes of contacting his dead daughter. Another writer, Sir Arthur Conan Doyle, the creator of Sherlock Holmes, became in later life a noted Spiritualist and spent a great deal of time investigating spiritual manifestations. At the time of his death, the inventor Thomas Edison was working on a machine to communicate with the dead.

However, many people scoff at the thought of ghosts or haunted houses. But there is really nothing silly or unscientific about believing in them. Discarnate spirits are just one theory—maybe the most logical one in many circumstances—to explain certain "unexplainable" phenomena that occur in many houses and areas of the world.

Most areas of the United States can boast of having haunted houses. Even the White House has been subject to the occurrences of strange phenomena usually associated with such places.

Probably the most famous house of this sort in recent years was documented in a 1977 book called *The Amityville Horror*. It told of a house in Amityville, New York, that presumably was, and still is, the haunt of some very evil entities. This house, at 112 Ocean Avenue, had been the scene of the highly publicized DeFeo murders.

On the night of November 13, 1974, Ronald DeFeo took a high-powered rifle and killed all six members of his family. Throughout the trial, DeFeo insisted that he had heard voices in the house and thought that God was talking to him. His attorney entered a plea of insanity, but he was judged sane, convicted and sentenced to six consecutive life terms for first-degree murder.

When George and Kathy Lutz bought the house, they thought they had found the house of their dreams. But after twenty-eight terror-filled days of levitations, doors torn off hinges, and harassment by a strange hooded figure—among other things—they abandoned the house for good, leaving their furniture and most of their clothes behind.

Frederick County does not, to the best of our knowledge, possess a dwelling like the house at 112 Ocean Avenue. Nevertheless, there are some interesting and colorful haunted houses located in this area.

A local psychic told us of a haunted house on Ballenger Creek Pike that he was investigating. He believed that the spirit was of an evil nature, but because the family that lived there accepted it, the spirit did nothing to harm them. However, it would become enraged if anyone questioned its existence.

On one occasion, a man who drove in a car pool with the owner of the house arrived early and was offered a cup of coffee. The family was discussing recent ghostly occurrences, and their guest was astonished that they believed in such foolishness. They cautioned the man not to treat the subject lightly or he would be subject to the spirit's wrath.

A short time later, as the men were driving to work, a huge fireball appeared in the car. The driver immediately stopped and the men attempted to get out, but they could not. They were trapped. The doors, though unlocked, would not open.

The driver suddenly looked at his companion and expressed his belief that the ghost did exist. At that moment, the fire was extinguished and the men continued on their way.

It is interesting to note how strange phenomena often occur in houses where a violent act has taken place. There is an old house near Lake Linganore in which a slave girl is believed to have been raped and murdered many years ago.

On at least one occasion, the present owner has been attacked by an unseen force. His legs were scratched repeatedly until they bled.

In the room where the rape and murder are thought to have taken place, there is a bloody handprint on the wall. Apparently, no amount of paint will cover it for long. The hand-shaped smudge always reappears within a short time.

A resident of Amelung Estates was sleeping quite soundly after a very trying day. Her two small sons had been particularly tiresome, romping through the house and getting into mischief. Suddenly, she was awakened by the sound of a child shrieking in the night, calling "Mama, Mama!" She raced to the next room, not knowing what she would find. Much to her surprise, her children were sleeping peacefully. Nothing would indicate that the cries had come from them. Yet, she felt they were real. She hadn't dreamt them. Where had the strange cries come from?

It wasn't until some years later that the housewife learned of others having similar experiences in Amelung Estates, a development in the southern part of the county.

The development was started after the completion of an archaeological dig conducted in 1963 and 1964. The dig was conducted in order to learn as much as possible about the American Glass Manufactory, completed on the site in 1789. The glass factory was built by Frederick Amelung shortly after he arrived in America from Bremen, Germany. Amelung and about 300 skilled immigrants built the factory and community of New Bremen. Very little of the community and factory remained, but those conducting the dig were successful in learning about Amelung's process and the everyday lives of the members of the New Bremen community. Unfortunately, they were unsuccessful in their attempt to locate the cemetery.

Sometime before the housewife's experience, she and her husband watched a stray dog carry a bone from a pile of dirt near their home. Later, two human skulls were found. The two human remains unearthed in this particular spot were approximately two hundred years old and were identified as a man of about 36 and a boy of 5 or 6. Apparently, they had found the long sought after graveyard.

It was after this unearthing that the eerie events started in several homes of Amelung Estates.

One resident of the development was repeatedly awakened by the screams of a child in the night. Each time she went to her daughter's room she found the child sleeping soundly. Later, after falling asleep on the sofa, she was awakened by what sounded like children's blocks being dropped into a box. Again she checked her child's room. As before, she found nothing but a sleeping child.

Another resident had a similar experience, but each time she checked on her children, she found that the night light in the bathroom had been turned off. At the time that the incidents occurred, she believed that her children were responsible. Finally, she entered her oldest child's room and demanded that the tricks be stopped. The child awoke, protesting her innocence, and then asked if she could please sleep somewhere else, because someone kept pushing her out of bed.

Several other families in the development have also experienced this "Child Ghost of Amelung"—possibly the ghost of the child whose bones were unearthed and examined at site of the New Bremen cemetery.

Landon is a large, historic home located near Urbana. It

contains 20 rooms, is 100 feet long and 39 feet wide.

The historic mansion was originally located on the shores of the Rappahannock River in Virginia, where it is thought to date back to 1754. Moved to its present site in 1846, it is believed to have been disassembled and taken by boat to Georgetown, completing its journey to Urbana by ox cart.

During the Civil War, Landon was used as a convalescent home for both Union and Confederate forces. Still visible on the study walls are the signatures of some of the soldiers treated there as well as sketches of Davis, Stuart, Lincoln and Grant.

In 1862, Landon served briefly as the headquarters of General J. E. B. Stuart, until overtaken by northern troops.

During this time, Stuart was accompanied by a Colonel Luke Tiernan Brien, his chief of staff. Brien, a native of Frederick County, liked the area so much that almost 20 years after the war he and his wife purchased 180 acres of rich farm land surrounding Landon, calling their estate Tyrone.

Since the deaths of the Briens in the early 1900's, there are those who say that Landon is haunted. Porch rockers move for no explainable reason, and on occasion an old man has been seen walking in the basement.

Recently, while in the basement, the grown son of the present owner and a friend were frightened by the appearance of the upper torso and head of an old man floating about.

The old man is believed to be the ghost of Colonel Brien.

However, Mrs. Brien is usually the more visible of the two. Children are often tucked into bed and when questioned, they insist that an old woman wearing a shawl was in their room. On one occasion, the young daughter of a house guest was even served a glass of milk.

Those hearing of incidents such as these can well believe that the Briens still *occupy* their lovely estate.

17

The Ghost of A. B. Nebb

In the early summer of 1970, a young couple and their two small children moved into an old, two-story house near the Frederick Fairgrounds.

Like most young couples in their first home, they enjoyed many hours decorating the house and working in the yard.

One day the wife was hanging curtains in the children's bedroom when she heard footsteps coming up the stairs and the words "Hi honey" coming from the doorway. Expecting to see her husband, she turned to find no one there.

Many other strange incidents soon followed.

They returned from trips to find furniture rearranged. Locked doors opened by themselves. They often heard voices in empty rooms and phantom footsteps on the stairs.

Paperboys were frightened by strange noises. Guests were often startled by loud crashes and what sounded like heavy objects rolling overhead. Baby sitters seldom lasted more than one night.

They felt their house was surely haunted, but decided they were not going to be scared away by any ghost. They continued remodeling the house and working in the yard, unaware the worst was yet to come.

One evening, while she was fixing dinner, she heard a deep moaning coming from beneath her. She thought something terrible had happened to her husband. She rushed downstairs and found him sitting at his desk. He had dropped his pencil and had both hands on his papers. He was just sitting there rigid, staring straight ahead. They looked at each other, and a chill ran up their spines.

That same night, the whole family was awakened by a loud crashing noise, which sounded like their pet dog was being thrown repeatedly against the back door. Almost immediately she began making a terrible howling sound. By the time they got there, the crashing noise had stopped, and their dog lay shaking and scared by the door.

Several weeks later, after they had all gone to bed, the young wife was awakened by what sounded like a child sobbing. She immediately checked the boy's bedroom and found both of them asleep. She started back, thinking it was only a dream, when she heard a strange noise at the end of the hall. The bathroom door was closed, and the light was off. Hearing nothing, she opened the door and turned on the light. She was startled to see a middle-aged man with dark curly hair, dressed in coveralls and boots, standing in the middle of the room. He looked directly at her and said, "Stop the digging; leave my family alone!" and then vanished.

Out of desperation, the young wife decided to try using a ouija board to contact whatever it was that was disrupting their lives. She convinced a neighbor to help her.

They placed their hands on the pointer and waited. They were amazed when it started to move.

The board told of a man named A. B. Nebb who had lived in an old shack nearby with his wife and small child some time in the last century. During an epidemic, his wife and child died, leaving him alone. He died a few years later, but every day he was alive he stopped by the graves of his wife and child. According to the board, A. B. Nebb still looks over the graves and will haunt anyone who disturbs them.

It didn't take long for them to realize that the gardening and digging in one part of the yard usually resulted in strange and frightening activities in the house. They moved their garden to another part of the yard and kept their dog chained to the back of the house. Much to their surprise, most of the ghostly activity stopped.

The past few years have been relatively quiet. Some ghostly activity still occurs, but it no longer frightens them. They still don't know if anyone is buried in the backyard, and no one wants to find out.

A Woodsboro Ghost

Woodsboro is a small rural community located about ten miles northeast of Frederick. It is a community steeped in tradition, as many of its residents are said to be descendants of the town's early settlers. Approaching Woodsboro from Walkersville—a rather scenic drive up Route 194—the first thing you notice is the Mount Hope Cemetary on the right. The town that follows is made up mostly of large shade trees and old Victorian homes—some of which are haunted.

One such house, located midway through town, has been haunted for at least ten years. Most of the time, the ghost is fairly tame. It is usually content just to open doors and curtains, and sing in the kitchen. But every now and then, something a little more startling happens.

The present owner, Elizabeth, has been frightened more than one night by slamming doors and bloodcurdling screams. Lately she has been awakened by strange scratching noises on her bedroom door.

One evening while Elizabeth was smoking a cigarette in the kitchen, she was startled by the sound of the latch lifting on the door leading to the upstairs hallway. As she watched, the door opened slowly and she became aware of a human shape taking form on the stairs. She had no desire to meet this spectre and quickly slammed the door and left the room.

Probably the most frightening experience occurred, for the first time, several months ago, and has happened again just recently. One night, while trying to sleep, Elizabeth sensed a presence in the room and then felt the edge of the bed lower, as though someone were sitting down. All she could do was keep her eyes tightly closed and pray until it went away.

Other people, too, have experienced the ghost and several have even seen it.

One elderly lady, spending the night, had awakened and started to get out of bed when she saw what appeared to be a young woman with long black hair dressed in a white gown lying on the floor. Almost immediately, the apparition rose and stood before her. She couldn't get out of the room fast enough. The terrified woman spent the rest of the night locked in the bathroom and has never spent a night in the house since.

Just who the ghost is no one knows for sure, but there are some interesting theories.

One local psychic who visited the house, believes the ghost is the daughter of a cruel man who lived in the area some years ago. According to the psychic, she had hated her father so that when she died of diphtheria, her ghost stayed around to torment him. She bothered him so much that he eventually hanged himself from a large tree in what is now Elizabeth's back yard. According to the psychic, it is the hatred for her father that keeps her there still.

Though neighbors do confirm that a man hanged himself in the back yard many years ago, former owners believe the ghost may be that of an elderly lady who died in the kitchen. They referred to their ghost as "Miss Molly", whom they often heard singing in the kitchen. The singing was often accompanied by the smell of perfume. It is interesting to note that to this day, many strange occurrences still happen in the kitchen.

Though Elizabeth is sometimes frightened by the

ghost, and her home is often in need of repair, she refuses to leave her Victorian surroundings. Apparently, the ghost, just like the faulty plumbing, has become just another problem to live with.

LEGENDS
AND
FOLKLORE

Ghosts And Legends

One of the most famous legends—of a supernatural nature—in American folklore is "The Legend of Sleepy Hollow." It recounts the amusing adventures of one Ichabod Crane and a headless horseman. This story first appeared in a larger work by Washington Irving, called *The Sketch-Book,* that also included the well known legend of Rip Van Winkle. This work is a collection of some of the best Eastern American folklore, mostly from Irving's home state of New York.

Generally speaking, legends are stories of people and/or events that are transmitted orally from one generation to another. Many may even have some basis in fact. Folklore includes legends, but also has broader meanings to include the customs, beliefs and traditions of a people.

Frederick County, too, abounds in tales of supernatural happenings—stories of gentlemanly ghosts, phantom buggies and bleeding tombstones. Though some may not be considered folklore in the strictest sense, almost all have been told or written about in the area for many years. What follows in this section is a selection of some of the more widely known *legends* of Frederick County.

One moonlit evening around the turn of the century, two well-thought of residents of East Prospect were driving their buggy somewhere in the New Windsor area. Suddenly, up ahead, as bright as day, they saw a mysterious looking buggy traveling in the same direction. As they were about to catch up with it, the vehicle suddenly disappeared. Their experience was not unique, however. The ghostly buggy was said to have been seen by others, under similar circumstances, in about the same area.

There is a legend about a gravestone that bleeds up Thurmont way. It seems that some years ago a man was involved in a tragic accident and buried. Apparently the man wasn't really dead and frantically tried to scratch and claw his way out of the grave, causing his fingers to bleed. The more he scratched, the more he bled; eventually, so legend has it, the man bled to death. Now there are dark stains on the tombstone all year round, and each year on the anniversary of his death, the tombstone turns red and drips blood.

In the eighteenth century Prospect Hall was one of the most beautiful estates in the county. Built in 1732 by Daniel Dulaney as a private home, the colonial mansion, located just outside of Frederick, now serves as a private school.

There is an interesting legend associated with the Dulaneys when they lived there many years ago.

It seems Daniel Dulaney's son, who at the time was 22 and of an amorous nature, shocked his family by falling in love with the pretty daughter of the housekeeper, a mulatto slave. The family would have no part of this, and his father immediately sent the young lad off to England.

Legend has it that Dulaney then boarded the girl up in a wall of the mansion and left her to die of suffocation.

Later owners claimed to hear muted knockings on the wall and someone walking about, though nothing or no one could be found.

Now the girl's pretty ghost is said to wander the corridors of Prospect Hall—occasionally startling students by opening and closing doors—waiting for her lost lover to return.

Many college students take great pleasure in spinning tales of horror to frighten their friends. These modern-day tales, re-told and embellished from year to year, are re-counted with some variations on campuses all over the country.

Not to be outdone, Frederick's own Hood College boasts its share of these stories.

An elevator in one of the dorms frequently goes up and down late at night, unoccupied.

Brodbeck Hall, built on the sight of a saloon, is often invaded at night by the laughter of dance hall girls and the coarse conversation of drinking men.

Of a more sinister nature is the story of the student whose throat was slit while she was alone, ironing in the basement. She somehow managed to make her way up three flights of stairs and wake her roommate before dying in the doorway of her room.

Auburn, a colonial mansion twelve miles north of Frederick near Catoctin Furnace, was built in 1808 by Baker Johnson, a brother of the first Governor of Maryland. It was later bought by the McPhersons and was their family home for over a hundred years. Standing on an elevation with a beautiful view of the valley, Auburn is quite impressive. It stands three stories high and contains many large rooms and hallways. The mansion is surrounded by a lovely landscape, dotted with large, radiant shade trees, with a shimmering lake to one side. It is here—at Auburn—that the ghost of Edward McPherson is said to wander.

Edward was about twenty years old when the war with Mexico began. His older brother William, a doctor, was about to enlist when Edward decided to take his place, as he thought the area needed his brother more than him. While serving as a first lieutenant in the army of General

Winfield Scott at Camp Mior in Mexico, Edward apparently quarrelled with a Lieutenant Maddox. They decided to duel, and on March 16, 1847, at age 22, Edward was mortally wounded. Within eight hours, Edward was dead.

Before he died he requested that his body be sent home. In those days, bodies were preserved by immersing them in whiskey. Apparently Edward returned home in a barrel full of spirits, inspiring one of his ancestors to remark, "What a waste of whiskey!"

Some time after his death, so the story goes, Edward's ghost began wandering the halls and stairways of Auburn. However, there was nothing frightening or evil about him. He would often greet guests and open doors for them. In fact, he was so polite and gentlemanly that he became affectionately known as "Sir" Edward.

There is a story that has been told around Frederick for some time about an elderly lady who lived with her daughter in what was one of the most beautiful estates in the area. It is said the old woman loved her home so much that she swore she would never leave.

One night, the old lady had a heart attack. Before she would go to the hospital, she insisted that her daughter help her change into her new shoes. As they were leaving, the old, worn out shoes were dropped by the fireplace in the living room.

The old woman died that same evening.

After the funeral, the daughter decided to sell the house and began clearing out the rooms. When she came to the living room, she saw her mother's old shoes on the hearth where she had dropped them.

She reached down to pick them up, but was unable to lift them. She tried with all her might, but they would not budge. Others tried, too. Legend has it that the shoes are there still.

The once beautiful estate is now deserted. It has not been lived in for over forty years, but no one will tear it

down. Though all the doors are boarded up, many people have reported seeing a strange figure enter the house at night and eerie lights emanating from it.

There are those who believe it is the old lady, who vowed never to leave.

There are many legends associated with war. One such legend dates back to the revolution after a Hessian defeat.

A group of captured Hessian soldiers was being taken by horse and sled to a federal prison located in Frederick, Maryland. The winter being bitter cold, the weary patriots, entrusted with the prisoners, decided to stop at a tavern near Gettysburg for a night's lodging. The Hessians were promptly locked in an upstairs bedroom, so the American soldiers could enjoy a night of drinking and merrymaking at the bar below.

As the evening wore on and the patriots grew more riotous, they became disillusioned with the responsibility of bringing the prisoners to Frederick. The thought of their poor, fledgling nation having to feed and clothe the captured soldiers for the length of the war was equally unappreciated. In their drunken state, they decided to kill their captives and be done with it.

Slowly, they marched up the stairs and slaughtered all of their prisoners. The bodies were thrown outside through the bedroom window and buried nearby.

A short time afterwards, terrible blood-curdling screams, shrieks of agony, and cries for mercy could be heard emanating from the tavern late at night—usually centering around the upstairs bedroom. It was believed to be the captured Hessians, protesting their fate.

It wasn't long before the tavern was abandoned—a place truly to be avoided.

Some years later, a group of young men out on a lark decided to spend the night in the old, abandoned tavern. The bravest members of the foolhardy group bedded down in the same upstairs bedroom that had witnessed the terrible carnage many years earlier. To further show their courage, they moved a heavy bureau against the door.

No sooner had they laid down to rest, than the horrible shrieks and cries began. Suddenly, the heavy bureau moved away from the door, prompting the frightened young men to quickly open the bedroom window to facilitate their escape. The discordant screams were of such a nature that one young man decided to dive rather than drop from the two-story window, breaking his leg in the fall. The young men would never go near the old tavern again.

Years later, some old human bones were excavated from a spot near where the tavern once stood. Possibly, these were the remains of the murdered Hessian soldiers, whose anguished cries once could be heard in the dead of night.

THE NEWEY SLAUGHTER

The neighbors were quickly summoned, but when they arrived, the house was fully engulfed in flames. An attempt at rescue was impossible. By the time the fire was extinguished, it was too late for the occupants still in the house. The grim search for the victims began—victims not of fire, but of brutal murder. For as the searchers were soon to discover, the Newey's had all been viciously mutilated. The children, Ann and Ruth; Mrs. Newey's father, Mr. Tresslar; the indentured servant, John Coombs; and John and Lydia Newey and their unborn child—all dead.

In 1825, John Newey finally realized that he could no longer tolerate his nephew's thievery and had him arrested. In the past, he had overlooked John Markley's abuses of his hospitality and compassion. But not this time. His nephew had stolen a wedding suit, a watch, and a large amount of cash.

In October, John Markley was convicted of theft and sentenced to five years in prison. As he was being taken from the courtroom, he swore he would get even with his uncle.

As the prison term drew to a close, many of John Newey's friends became concerned for his safety because they knew Markley well enough to realize he was sitting in his cell planning his revenge.

December 29, 1830, was a busy day on the Newey farm. The entire family, along with many friends and neighbors were butchering that day. Late that afternoon, the youngest of the Neweys' daughters was sent to the barn to gather eggs. When she returned, she told of seeing a stranger near the barn. Everyone was so busy that the child's words were soon forgotten.

Finally, the work was completed. One of the neighbors, Mrs. Flautt, was invited to stay the night, but she refused. She was reminded of the child's report of the stranger, and she wished to get away from the farm as quickly as possible.

Even after returning home she could not dispel her concern. Sleep eluded her and she finally got out of bed. As soon as she gazed out the window, she knew her worst fears were true. There, in the distance, John Newey's house stood engulfed in flames.

The recovered bodies were prepared for burial immediately, but the ground was so frozen that the graves were quite shallow. Several days later the bodies had to be exhumed for medical examination and were then re-buried in the same unmarked graves.

John Markley was arrested in Hagerstown a few days later. Items in his possession at the time of his arrest were positively identified as property of the Neweys.

Markley insisted he was innocent—but became the first person convicted of murder on circumstantial evidence in the state.

It was believed that there had to have been an accomplice, but there was no proof. In Ohio, many years later, a man claimed to have been Markley's accomplice. Apparently he couldn't die in peace without confessing the ghastly crimes he helped commit.

On June 21, 1831, Markley was hanged on Barrick's Hill. Three companies of militia were required to control the crowd that had traveled to Frederick that day to witness the execution.

For years they talked about the bloody murders of the Newey family that took place that New Years Eve, in the Harbaugh Valley of Maryland. It is said that descendants of the family, who remain in the area, still remember their grandparents telling of those awful killings that occurred that winter's night in 1830.

No house stands on the Newey property now—just the cellar and scattered debris, and no headstones mark the mass grave. But if you pass by the property on a cold winter's night, do not be surprised if you see a strange man wearing old work clothes sneaking around the area. Only a few people have seen him, but the description fits one man perfectly—John Markley.

And the solitude of the landscape may be shattered by the crackle of a raging fire or by the terrified screams of the Newey family as they struggle and cry in vain for their lives.

A Christmas Legend

In Emmitsburg, something of a legend has grown up around a former flute player named Larry Dielman, who has been dead for over fifty years.

Music was in his blood from the very beginning. His father, Professor Casper Dielman, had been a noted composer and musician in Germany in the early 1800's. He came to America where he wrote inauguration marches for four presidents and led symphony orchestras in New York, Philadelphia, and Baltimore before settling in Emmitsburg to teach music at St. Mary's College in 1834.

It was here in Emmitsburg, in 1838, that Larry was born. His father had high hopes for him as a classical musician, but Larry never quite measured up.

Though he grew up in the shadow of his father, his younger days were for the most part gay and happy. Larry and the professor spent many fun-filled evenings at home entertaining guests with their musical compositions. As he grew older, he became quite popular with the college crowd, and enjoyed entertaining them. His colorful personality and flamboyant wardrobe attracted many of them to his small grocery store near the college. There, sitting on the porch, he would often make up songs on the spur of the moment and sing them to the pretty girls.

In his twenties, Larry found and married the girl of his dreams and settled down to a joyful life. The joy soon turned to bitterness, however, and his young wife left him. There was now a touch of sadness to Larry's life that was never to leave it. Those few residents who still remember him recall the figure of a lonely old man sitting on the porch of his store with his banjo, singing of his long-lost love.

In 1885, the old professor died, and it was a sad Larry Dielman who took his flute to the cemetery to play the following Christmas. As the strains of *When the Glory Lit the Midnight Air,* one of his father's most famous compositions, cascaded down from the grave, the people of Emmitsburg thought he had finally mastered the flute in memory of his father. The town folk donned their coats and hats and made the steep journey to the gravesite by the Grotto of Our Lady of Lourdes.

The event became a tradition. Every year thereafter, Larry Dielman would' lead a procession up the steep hill to the tiny gravesite and play beautiful, lilting music. In 1900, when the congregation moved from. St. Mary's to St. Anthony's, where midnight Mass was held on Christmas Eve, Larry played at night as well as in the morning.

In later years, he was unable to make the steep climb and had to be taken by sled. Finally, in 1923, Larry Dielman died.

Oldtimers say that if you listen very carefully on Christmas Eve or Christmas morning you can still hear the ethereal strains of beautiful flute music floating down from the cemetery. A short time later, it is gone, not to be heard again for another year.

THE
CIVIL
WAR

CIVIL WAR SPOOKS

When one thinks of Frederick's part in the Civil War, the name Barbara Fritchie immediately comes to mind. An elderly, opinionated woman was immortalized by John Greenleaf Whittier's account of an event many historians argue never happened.

Historians do agree, however, that Frederick County played an important part in the Civil War. In October of 1859, word was received that John Brown and his raiders had captured the arsenal at Harper's Ferry. The first offer of assistance accepted by President Buchannan was that of Frederick's military companies.

On July 9, 1864, the City of Frederick was forced to pay a ransom of $200,000 to General Jubal A. Early. The delay caused by the negotiations for the ransom allowed the Union forces to form a line of defense and prepare for the Battle of the Monocacy. This battle was doubly important, because it allowed the Union army to fortify and successfully defend Washington, D.C., and force the Rebels into Virginia.

During the Civil War, troops of both armies crossed the state innumerable times. At one point, Frederick County had as many as seventeen hospitals treating wounded Union troops and Confederate prisoners. Many area homes were commandeered as headquarters buildings for both armies.

Some Frederick County families were sympathetic to the Confederate cause. One such family welcomed a wounded Rebel soldier into their home. When a company of Union troops appeared, the young soldier was hidden in the cellar. The soldiers were expected to take what supplies they needed and leave. Unfortunately for the young man, they did not. The company set up their camp right in the front yard and stayed for several weeks. With all the excitement, the family completely forgot about their other "guest." Finally, after the passage of several months, he was remembered. When they went to the cellar, all they found were his bones.

After the discovery of the skeleton, moaning and scratching sounds were heard in the cellar, and visitors were often startled by the sudden appearance of a young man dressed in the uniform of a Confederate soldier.

On September 10th, the armies of Generals Lee, Jackson, and Longstreet began to march west across Frederick County. They would be forced to retreat from South Mountain on September 14th, after a costly battle.

There were many such costly battles for the Confederates in Frederick County. One such battle occurred on the outskirts of Burkittsville, just below what is now a memorial to Civil War correspondents.

Incredible as it may seem, both armies decided to add an element of surprise by striking before dawn. But as the Confederate troops began the time-consuming task of moving their cannon up the hill, the Union troops, armed only with rifles, took the Rebels entirely by surprise. Many of the Southern troops retreated, but thousands of them fell before sunrise.

For many years, there have been reports of strange sightings and occurrences in that area. Occasionally, eerie campfires can be seen in the mountains and open fields. Phantom soldiers appear to be sitting before a fire warming themselves. Upon closer investigation, the strange scene vanishes.

One of the strangest and most difficult occurrences to explain takes place just before you reach Burkittsville at a spot now known as *Spook Hill*. If you stop the motor of your car and place it in neutral, you will suddenly feel as if you are being pulled back up the hill, upon leaving town, you will feel as though you are being pushed. It is believed by many that the car is being moved by the spirits of the dead soldiers continuing to perform their duties.

Anyone who has journeyed to Burkittsville and experienced the sensation of moving uphill, can well believe that phantom soldiers are struggling to move the car *just as they struggled with the cannon many years ago.*

Another area landmark, dating back to the early part of the nineteenth century, is believed to be the home of Civil War spirits.

In 1807, Leonard Harbaugh began building a stone bridge in Frederick County. After its completion, he built a large *demijohn* alongside the bridge. At that time it was believed that a bottle of whiskey was sealed inside the jug. Civil War soldiers were also believed to use the jug as a hiding place for their whiskey.

Passers-by frequently reported hearing many strange sounds in the area of the jug. Even after the old bridge collapsed and was replaced, the strange sounds followed the jug to its new location.

Restless spirits, possibly those of young men killed during one of the many battles fought in this area, are believed to continue to search for the whiskey they placed in the jug so many years ago.

An Old Wise Tale

Early one evening, Mr. Wise was sitting on his porch smoking his pipe when he saw a man dressed in a gray uniform coming up the road from Middletown. As the man drew closer, he appeared to be gliding along the road, his feet not quite touching the ground. Suddenly, old Mr. Wise sat up and stared. He could see clear through the man. As the man approached, Wise heard him say, "I've come to have you turn me over, Mr. Wise, that's all I want done."

Wise was frozen to his chair, unable to speak.

The apparition continued, "Why not? You threw me down the well. I was the last man in and you'll find me right on top. I'm very uncomfortable down there, lying on my face. Really, Mr. Wise, I can't rest—I can't get my breath."

"How can that be! You were dead when I put you in!"

Wise knew very well where the soldier was buried. After the battle of South Mountain, he was paid five dollars per man to bury the dead. Eager to have the money, but reluctant to perform the service, he quickly placed as many bodies as possible in an abandoned well on a nearby farm. One of the men he buried was Sergeant Jim Tabbs of Virginia, the soldier he now faced.

"That's true—I am dead," replied the soldier, "but I'm uncomfortable just the same. I've come all this way

just to have you turn me, Mr. Wise. If you don't, I'll come back every night until you do."

"You'll do it tonight, won't you Mr. Wise? I can't rest in peace 'til I'm turned over."

"I'll do it! I'll do it if it kills me!" It would be an unpleasant task, but if he wanted any peace he would have to turn the body over.

Satisfied that Wise would comply with his request, Jim turned and walked down the road. Just as he disappeared the frightened old man heard, "Remember, Mr. Wise, I've got to be turned over. I'll come back every night 'til you turn me or you're dead."

Wise finally went to bed, but was unable to sleep, his mind filled with thoughts of the dead soldier. Just before sunrise, he took his spade and went to the well. The well was dry. It was now the final resting place for almost fifty Confederate soldiers.

Driven by the fear of what would happen if he did not keep his promise, Wise began digging. At last he reached the first body and found that it was Jim Tabbs lying on his face. He reached down and tugged until he turned the body over, straightened it as best he could, and replaced the earth over the grave.

Greatly relieved, Wise picked up his shovel and hurried home, never mentioning his ordeal to anyone.

Unfortunately, he was soon visited by more trouble related to the mass grave. The authorities discovered the location and circumstances of the burial of the Confederate soldiers and forced Wise to provide a proper grave for each soldier.

The ghosts of Jim Tabbs and his company of Virginians were finally at peace, and Jim never returned to the Wise cabin.

THE PHANTOM BATTLE

It was Halloween. The air was cool, the sky clear and bright. All but two of the guests at South Mountain House were asleep. Both men were reading in their rooms, relaxing after a day of traveling.

Suddenly, one of the guests became aware of a sulphurous odor coming from the direction of the barn. Thinking that a vagrant had started a fire to ward off the night's chill, he ran to his window to investigate. Sure enough, he could see wisps of smoke coming from the direction of the barn, and the smell was even more distinct. Not wanting to awaken the entire household, he went to the room of one of the other guests, and informed him of his suspicions. They proceeded to the observatory at the top of the house, where the smoke was even more apparent.

The two men went immediately to the servants' quarters and sent a man-servant to investigate. After some time, he returned and informed the guests that he had checked the barn and all the other out-buildings on the property and had found no sign of fire anywhere. The servant, annoyed at the interruption of his sleep, returned to his room, leaving the two guests perplexed. The men, confused by the servant's report, returned to the observatory. The smoke was still visible.

Suddenly, at the stroke of twelve, an unbelievable event occurred.

The smoke took on the eerie shape of men. Columns

of phantom soldiers converged upon the summit and met in fierce combat. The air was filled with the odor of cannon and gunpowder. The terrified men ran into the house and slammed the door. As the door slammed, the battle ended and the soldiers disappeared.

On September 13, 1862, Union forces drove Stuart's Confederate Cavalry from strong positions on Catoctin Mountain across the Middletown Valley to South Mountain at Turner's Gap, where Hill's forces were forming defensive positions.

The Battle of South Mountain began on the morning of the 14th, when Hill's troops attempted to halt the Union army at Catoctin Creek. It was an unsuccessful effort, and they were forced to retreat further up the mountain. The Confederates were outflanked on the right and the left by the troops of Generals Cox, Reno, Hooker and Ricketts, and by evening were forced to retreat, leaving their dead and wounded among the corn fields and pine trees of South Mountain. By days end, more than one thousand men were lost.

The sounds of the battle could be heard in Frederick, and the sulphurous smell of cannon and gunpowder permeated the air.

Could these two men, brought together by chance at an inn on the National Pike, have witnessed the agony of those men who had died in battle almost twenty years before?

If so, they were not alone. Fifty years later, two travelers on the Appalachian Trail chose to camp in the field beneath South Mountain House. They fell asleep almost immediately, but were awakened around eleven by what sounded like clashing swords. The night air was filled with a sulphurous odor and the sounds moved closer. Suddenly, two columns of soldiers faced each other in battle. They disappeared after a few minutes, and South Mountain became peaceful again. Peaceful to all but the two frightened campers, who would never rest easy on South Mountain again.

STRANGE
CREATURES

GHOST DOGS

Most areas of the world have their accounts of strange creatures. Several come to mind quite easily—the Abominable Snowman of the Himalayas and Bigfoot of the Pacific Northwest. Not to be left out, Frederick County, too, has had its share of strange animals. Tales of the Dwayyo and the Snallygaster have amused Frederick Countians for many years. Less well known are the accounts of numerous four-legged *friends*.

Probably the most famous dog of this sort is the Snarly Yow or Black Dog. He was often seen in the last century on South Mountain coming down a favorite path toward the National Pike, now Alternate Route 40. Here, he would sometimes stop, scaring any passing travelers, before continuing his journey down the mountain. Any attempts made to follow the strange beast would usually result in the dogs sudden disappearance.

It is interesting to note how accounts of strange animals are often associated with the deaths of cruel men. There was such a man who lived in the Urbana district on an estate called Addison in the 1830's, a slave owner named Singleton Burgee. That the slaves despised Singleton was common knowledge, and they took great pleasure in initiating stories about him, probably leading to the

51

belief that Addison is now haunted. On his deathbed, it is said a strange man wearing a black cape and riding a black horse came to Singleton's house. As he stood over Singleton's bed, he chanted, "Are you ready, Singleton Burgee?", then vanished. Three days before Singleton died, a strange black dog appeared on the steps leading to the room where he lay. The dog kept the strange vigil until Singleton Burgee was dead, then it too vanished.

Another strange dog, seen in the Emmitsburg area, is said to be the ghost of a cruel landowner named Leigh Masters. Apparently the dog has been sited in the Emmitsburg region for over one hundred years.

In 1887, two men were riding at dusk near Ore Mine Bridge when suddenly a large black dog came *through* a fence on one side of the road. The two men watched aghast as the strange animal crossed the path in front of them and then passed through a fence on the other side.

There have been other apparent sitings. Once, a man tried to strike the creature with a whip, only to see it go right through. Another man claimed it had intelligence, for when he spoke to the dog, "Come here and walk beside me," it did. A man driving a wagon once reported a large black dog wearing a chain walked beside his wagon for about one hundred yards and then vanished.

The strange black dog is said to be about three feet tall, usually seen with a huge chain around its neck. Legend has it that the strange animal is never seen more than once by the same person.

Rose Hill Manor is an historic, two hundred year old mansion located in the northern part of Frederick. Once owned and lived in by the first governor of Maryland, Thomas Johnson, the former estate is now owned by the county and serves as museum for children.

It is reputedly haunted by many ghosts, one of which is the blue ghost of an old dog that sometimes wanders the grounds at midnight.

The story is told of a wealthy man who lived there many years ago with only his dog for company. Not one to trust in banks, he buried all his money somewhere on the property. In his will, he left directions where to find it, presumably six feet from an old oak tree. After he died, many people searched the estate for the buried treasure, but no one has been successful.

Some nights, the old blue dog can be seen roaming the grounds and on occasion has been heard to bark. It is believed if the dog can be followed while barking, its pursuer will be led to the buried gold. However, the ghostly blue dog always disappears before any treasure can be found.

THE SNALLYGASTER

Reports of a strange, flying beast known as the Snally-gaster first appeared in Frederick County in early February, 1909. The story was carried prominently in Middletown's *Valley Register,* a weekly newspaper, for about a month, when the story mysteriously died.

In the early issues, the flying beast seemed to be everywhere at once: New Jersey, West Virginia, Ohio, *and headed this way.*

It was reported to have created quite a stir in New Jersey, where its footprints were first discovered in the snow.

The first person to see it, James Harding, described it as having enormous wings, a long sharp beak, claws like steel, and one eye in the middle of its forehead. He said it made shrill screeching noises and looked like a cross between a tiger and a vampire.

A vampire may have been a good description, for it was reported to have killed a colored man, Bill Gifferson, by piercing his neck with its sharp bill and slowly sucking his blood.

It was also seen in West Virginia, where it almost caught a woman near Scrabble, roosted in Alex Crows's barn, and laid an egg near Sharpsburg, where it was reported some men had rigged up an incubator to try to hatch it.

T. C. Harbaugh, of Casstown, Ohio, wrote a letter to the *Valley Register* in early 1909, telling of a strange beast that flew over his area making terrible screeching noises. Harbaugh described it as having two huge wings, a large horny head, and a tail twenty feet long. He said it looked as though it was headed this way.

Sure enough, the Snallygaster was first sighted in Maryland by a colored man, who fired a brick-burning kiln near Cumberland. The strange beast was seen cooling its wings over the outlet of the kiln. When the beast's sleep was disturbed by the man, it emitted a blood-curdling scream and angrily flew away.

It was also shot at near Hagerstown, sighted south of Middletown at Lover's Leap, and seen flying over the mountains between Gapland and Burkittsville, where it was reported to have laid another egg—big enough to hatch an elephant.

Sightings of the Snallygaster were creating such a commotion that at one point it was reported that President Theodore Roosevelt might postpone a trip to Europe so that he could lead an expedition to capture it.

Apparently the Smithsonian Institute was also interested in the beast. From the description provided by engineer 83, at Shepherdstown, West Virginia, they determined the strange beast was either a bovalopus or a Snallygaster, since it had the characteristics of both. Further, its hide was so rare that it was worth $100,000 a square foot, as it was the only substance known to man that could polish punkle shells.

Punkle shells, for those of you who don't know, are used by the African tribes of Umbopeland for ornamentation.

The last sighting in Frederick County in 1909, occurred near Emmitsburg in early March. Three men fought the terrible creature outside a railroad station for nearly an hour and a half before chasing it into the woods of Carroll County.

Twenty three years passed before the Snallygaster appeared again in Frederick County.

First reports were received from just below South Mountain in Washington County. Eyewitness accounts claimed that it flew toward them from the Middletown Valley.

The beast was often seen floating back and forth over the area and was described as being as large as a dirigible, with arms resembling the tentacles of an octopus. The creature appeared to be able to change its size, shape, and color at will.

Although the creature made no attempt to harm any of the residents of the Valley, most people sought the safety of their homes as it flew overhead.

All descriptions seemed to indicate it was *the Snally-gaster,* last reported in these parts on March 5, 1909. As the life expectancy of a Snallygaster is only about twenty years, the most logical explanation seemed to be that the latest sighting was the offspring of the 1909 creature, possibly hatched from one of the eggs layed near Burkittsville.

Since the Snallygaster appears so rarely, the Middletown *Valley Register* requested that local residents sighting the creature provide as accurate and detailed a description as possible for scientific purposes.

Two such residents, Charles F. Main and Edward M. L. Lighter, were able to provide the necessary information. While driving a truck on the National Pike, just east of Braddock Heights, they spotted the Snallygaster flying about twenty five feet overhead. They thoroughly confirmed the descriptions published the previous week.

The Snallygaster finally met his end in a way some might envy. The creature was flying near Frog Hollow in Washington County when it was attracted by the aroma of a 2500 gallon vat of moonshine. As the beast flew overhead, it was overcome by the fumes and dropped into the boiling mash. A short time later, revenue agents George Dansforth and Charles Cushwa arrived on the scene. They

had received information about the still, but were rather startled at the sight of the dead monster in the vat.

The two agents exploded five hundred pounds of dynamite under the still, destroying the remains of the Snallygaster and John Barleycorn's workshop.

A great deal has been written about the Snallygaster since 1909. It has appeared in countless articles in the Middletown *Valley Register, Frederick News Post,* and other area newspapers. It has also appeared in the *Baltimore Sun, National Geographic,* and *Time* Magazine.

In 1976, the *Washington Post* sponsored an unsuccessful search for the Snallygaster, as well as other strange Maryland creatures.

Frederick County is known for a great many things, but most will agree that none is as imaginative as the Snallygaster. Those of us who have been entertained by stories of the Snallygaster owe our thanks to the resourceful staff of the Middletown *Valley Register,* particularly George C. Rhoderick, Sr. and Ralph S. Wolfe, Sr., who in 1909 thought they would write a little nonsense to entertain the readers and boost circulation. Little did they realize that their imagination would continue to amuse for seventy years.

THE DWAYYO

On Saturday evening, November 27, 1965, near the woods of Gambrill State Park, "John Becker" went out in his yard to investigate a strange noise. It was getting dark, and he had started back to the house, when he saw it—something moving toward him.

"It was as big as a bear, had long black hair, a bushy tail, and growled like a wolf or a dog in anger."

As it got closer, it stood up on its hind legs and attacked him. "Becker" fought the creature until it ran into the woods, leaving him, his wife and children in horror.

Deciding to remain anonymous under the alias John Becker, he filed a report with local state police, telling of an attack by a mysterious monster that he called a *Dwayyo.*

Sensing a good story, *Frederick News Post* reporter George May wrote a series of articles on the monster, and soon newspapers throughout the area were carrying the story.

These articles spawned a rash of calls and letters to the newspaper, ranging from the absurd to the furious.

Several University of Maryland students wrote that they had investigated the origin of the unknown creature and had traced its ancestry to the upper Amazon River and the Yangtze River plateau. They also reported that they had seen several of the creatures on campus late at night and found them friendly and fun loving.

The County Treasurer's office recieved an application for a Dwayyo license from a "John Becker" accompanied by the one dollar fee. The license was issued and mailed in care of George May, *Frederick News Post.*

An Adamstown woman called the paper and insisted that "this trash about the Dwayyo be stopped." She said her daughter was being treatcd for a nervous condition because of all this talk about the Dwayyo.

The Frederick newspapers also reported other "sightings."

Several hunters saw a strange black beast roaming the woods. An Ellerton woman reported that residents of that area had heard something cry like a baby and scream like a woman for several months. A Jefferson woman said that she saw a strange dog-shaped animal about the size of a calf chasing some cows on a farm near her home.

However, investigations by local and state police turned up nothing substantial on the John Becker-Dwayyo srory.

By mid-December, the story started to fade. There had not been any sightings for several days, and it was suggested that the Dwayyo had moved on to another area.

For some people, the Dwayyo was a reminder of the Snallygaster—possibly even hatched from a Snallygaster egg. To others it was merely a case of premature Christmas *cheer.*

SOUTH
MOUNTAIN

SOUTH MOUNTAIN LEGENDS

Winding our way from Frederick, through the Middletown Valley, across beautiful rolling hills, we come to one of the ranges of the Blue Ridge chain that extends from Virginia to Pennsylvania: *South Mountain*. The scene of the bloody Civil War battle that raged all day on September 14, 1862, it has long been an historic place.

But more than just historic in interest, South Mountain has long been associated with strange stories, spooks, and legends—most dating back to the last century.

There are several accounts of a banshee called the White Woman who roamed South Mountain some years ago. Apparently, her appearance was very much dreaded, as it was considered a harbinger of death or some other disaster.

Annie was a simple young mountain girl, who lived in a hut with her grandmother and her Uncle Ike. One summer day, she was looking out on the road when she saw the White Woman. The shrouded figure arose from the surface of the road and then seemed to pass through the house. Two days later, Ike died, and not long afterward the hut burned to the ground.

Another time, the banshee was sighted by a woman who was caring for her nine-day old grandchild. The ghostly figure of the child's recently dead mother was seen bending over the cradle. Shortly thereafter, the baby died.

The White Woman was seen roaming South Mountain on several other occassions, though nothing harmful seemed to come of it.

One evening in 1817, a company of Army regulars on their way to fight the Seminole Indians, stopped at South Mountain House for a nights lodging.

Most of the men joined the local residents already in the bar for some pleasant conversation.

One soldier, a handsome young man from Michigan, remained in the kitchen near the fire, unable to take his eyes off the tavern keeper's young daughter, Saidee, as she prepared dinner.

He would regret having to leave her in the morning, for Cupid's arrow had pierced his heart. As Saidee turned to face him, he said, "Saidee, I wish that I could die for you!"

"Die for me," she said angrily. "Ain't I worth living for?"

At that the young man made his decision. He would desert and hide in the forest near the overhanging cliffs. Saidee agreed to bring him food and cry like a wildcat when danger was near. When it was safe for him to return, they would marry and build a cabin on the mountain.

His company searched for him for days, never even considering that he had deserted. Convinced that he was dead, the company departed, and the young soldier returned for Saidee. They married, lived and died on South Mountain.

Their story is still told, and some say the lovers are seen, their footsteps are heard, and the cry of a wildcat often breaks the silence of the night on South Mountain.

A young Frederick woman told of a terrifying childhood experience when she lived on South Mountain.

Residents of that area were often frightened at night by strange screaming noises. In the morning cats, chickens, and cattle were often found dead and many times eaten.

All attempts to hunt the unseen carnivore proved in vain. The young woman's father searched for it with a rifle until frightened away by its shrill cries. Dogs refused to hunt the strange animal and would hide under the porch if they sensed its presence.

Late one afternoon as she was climbing a tree, she spotted a strange creature coming down the hill to her left. It resembled a dog, with a face like a cat, and had a bristle-like hairy coat. She watched breathlessly as it moved in her direction, making a low murmuring sound. She leaped from the tree and ran toward her yard. Her screams must have frightened it, for when she turned, the strange beast had vanished. All that could be found were a few large tracks leading nowhere in the underbrush.

She swears her story is true, though she was the only one to ever see it.

Reports of this kind have not been unusual on South Mountain—where the young woman's story took place. Tales of a strange dog-like creature date back almost a century, when it was then called the Black Dog or Snarly Yow. We have already mentioned this vicious looking dog who would often confront and frighten passing travelers on the National Pike. It was usually described as having large paws, wolfish teeth, and an ugly red mouth.

Late one evening many years ago, William, a hard working and sober married man of about thirty, was returning home from an errand in Boonsboro. He was approaching the Glendale area of South Mountain when he encountered a strange black dog blocking his path. Fearlessly he lashed out at the beast, his fists striking only the air. The dog was bigger than any he had ever seen, but as he *fought* it, the beast grew to monsterous proportions, taking up the whole width of the road. Then, without a sound, the huge creature bared its teeth, exposing an ugly red mouth, and passed into the darkness, leaving William frightened and confused, but otherwise unharmed, to continue his journey home.

Another time, a man of considerable strength, whose thirst for whiskey equaled his size, was confronted by a huge black dog. The horse he was riding stopped dead in its tracks and couldn't be budged by verbal or physical abuse. Finally, the panicked horse reared up and threw his master to the ground, breaking his collar bone. The dog vanished as quickly as it had appeared.

A man known to be a crack shot with a rifle came upon the dog crossing the road. The marksman took steady aim and fired several shots. However, the bullets passed right through the undaunted beast, leading the rifleman to flee in terror.

Another area resident, nicknamed "Big Joe," encountered the Black Dog while riding his horse one evening. Joe pursued the animal for some distance but failed to overtake it. He insisted that as the dog ran, it kicked up dirt and gravel like any other large running animal— and then mysteriously disappeared.

In 1975, the strange dog was seen again, in the same area as former accounts. A group of sightseers returning to Middletown from Washington Monument State Park suddenly came upon the beast in their automobile. They heard the unmistakable thud and felt the impact of the animal being crushed under the wheels. The car was stopped and they were amazed to see the dog standing upright on its huge paws. The beast bared its teeth, showing an ugly red mouth, then vanished as suddenly as it had appeared.

THE SABBAT

Christian European tradition is rich in the lore of the sabbat—or witches sabbath—a nightly gathering of witches, wizards, and demons. Apparently the practice dates back to the Inquisition, although certain classical Roman authors wrote of such events. These horrid creatures would arrive by anointing themselves with a special ointment that allowed them to fly or by riding an animal provided by the devil. Once there they engaged in sacrilegious rites, much feasting and revelry, and worship of the devil.

Stories of the sabbat probably followed the immigrants to the New World where they were changed and embellished to fit the particular people and locale. One such story was told on South Mountain in the last century.

Many years ago, a wealthy farmer, having lived for some years in an old two-story log cabin, decided to build a new home for his large family.

The new house was solidly constructed of brick and was situated atop a hill in a way that it was protected from cold and wind at the edge of a grove of trees. That this spot was said to be haunted, a trysting place for demons, had left the family undaunted.

But from the very first night, they knew no peace. The house rang with demonic laughter, cries and groans. The mornings would find the family petrified. After a few weeks of this, they returned to their old log cabin, leaving a great deal of their furniture behind.

For months afterwards, lights were seen in the new home and the nighttime peace was often broken by unearthly sounds emanating from it. They felt they would never occupy their new home again.

Late one night during a particularly bad storm, a weary stranger knocked at the door and asked for lodging. Unfortunately, there was no room in the farmer's old log cabin.

Seeing the lights in the house on the hill, the traveler said he would try there. Upon hearing this, the frightened farmer offered the man the comfort of his barn, warning him that the house he saw was haunted.

The traveler said that he would go on and that God would protect him from evil spirits.

When he reached the house, the door flew open. Unafraid, he entered, climbed the stairs and found a comfortable room on the second floor. After praying, he locked the door and lay down. The luxury of sleep was not to be his. As soon as his head hit the pillow, the entire house was filled with noise as a large number of festive people suddenly arrived.

After a while, he heard footsteps on the stairs. Slowly, but deliberately, they advanced until reaching the entrance to his room.

The door flew open, and a distinguished looking man stood before him dressed in evening attire. He knew at once that he stood face-to-face with the Devil himself. Cast aside were the horns and cloven foot of the dark ages, replaced by a black dress suit, white tie, and boutonniere.

He graciously extended an invitation to a champagne supper, and the weary traveler promptly accepted.

The two men descended the stairs and entered a room hung with crystal chandeliers entwined with huge serpants.

A Lucullan display of delicacies covered a massive table.

The fine crystal goblets, cast in shapes to arouse passions, were filled with excellent wines and spirits, and the transparent china, skillfully portrayed all manner of debauchery.

All of the women present were beautifully attired in the latest fashion, bedecked with jewels, painted faces, beautifully coiffed hair and an all-pervading sense of evil.

So too, the men—elegantly dressed worshipers of evil.

After the guest was presented, the entire company sat in their appointed places to dine. As the guest took his place, he said that he would accept his host's hospitality on one condition—that he be allowed to offer thanks to God for such a fine meal. At this, the lights flickered, flames shot from the wine, the meat rotted, the people became old and decayed, and the air was filled with the odor of the grave.

The terrified traveler quickly made the sign of the cross, and in God's name commanded the demons to leave.

At that moment there was an explosion, followed by groans, screams and curses, and then, total darkness. The once lovely room was now filled with the sickening smell of sulpher, and the entire house shook as the burden of sin was lifted and the demons returned to the depths of hell.

After offering thanks to God, the traveler returned to the farmer's cabin. The farmer fell to his knees when the stranger returned, for he had heard the explosion and feared the man was dead.

At dawn, the house remained standing and unharmed, and the traveler continued on his journey.

The farmer and his family returned to their home and lived undisturbed, never forgetting to offer thanks to God.

WINGS AT MIDNIGHT

Late in the 1800's, South Mountain House—now a restaurant called *Old South Mountain Inn*—located about twelve miles northeast of Frederick, was poised atop South Mountain much like an old manor seat, then being the only building of any size for miles. Founded in 1732, as an inn for weary travelers, this old structure has had an interesting history. It is said that General Edward Braddock, accompanied by a young lieutenant named George Washington, marched his army past this old inn on his way to his death near Fort Duquesne in the French and Indian War. Later, in the 1820's, it served as a wagon stand and stage coach stop on the National Road, now Alternate Route·40. During the Civil War, the old inn was briefly held as an overnight outpost and staging point for some of John Brown's followers. Later, it was the headquarters of Confederate General D. H. Hill, during the battle of South Mountain.

South Mountain House, as we shall call it, is not only known for its history but for the strange stories and legends associated with it.

One night, many years ago, after an evening of pleasant conversation, one lady guest at South Mountain House was preparing for bed. It had been a long, wearying day, and the summer night seemed more oppressive than usual. She sat by the window, hoping to catch a last breath of

70

fresh, cool air before retiring. During the day, she had a magnificent view westward over fields which had once witnessed the dreadful scenes of war. Now the fields were dark and quiet.

Suddenly, she was startled by a bright light cast upon the house. Looking up, there was not a star visible, the sky inky black.

She glanced toward the field. Not over fifty yards away stood an apparition, an eight foot tall shrouded figure of human form. There was an eerie atmosphere of bright, white light that surrounded it. Not another look was taken, the window quickly closed.

She noted the time and perceived a sudden chill. It was the exact moment of midnight.

After some initial storytelling, the incident was scarcely spoken of again. The summer passed, and another had succeeded it, when one night the hostess heard a light tapping at her door. She opened it to find one of her guests standing nervously in the doorway.

"I am sorry to disturb you, madam," the woman said. "I have just seen a ghost!"

She was offerred a chair, and presently she told her story. She had not been there the summer before; nevertheless, she told practically the same eerie tale. She was standing by the window, when she saw a strange phantom about thirty yards from the house. She hurriedly looked away, but she couldn't help noticing the strange white light that seemed to emanate from it in all directions.

They agreed not to mention the incident to anyone, as the old English clock struck midnight.

Some weeks later, the lady's stay at South Mountain House was about to end. She was to leave early the next morning, and the hostess decided to see if anything could be done to make the following day's mountain drive more comfortable.

The hour was late, and the two ladies were reminded of the mysterious apparition that had appeared twice in

succeeding summers. They stood at the same open casement that looked out over the dark, mystic grove, where the phantom had been seen before. Suddenly, involuntarily, one of them leaned out the window and shouted into the darkness: "Who are you? Are you a lost soul?"

Scarcely an instant later, two phosphorescent wings flashed and fluttered wildly in the grove a few yards away. Then, suddenly, the two wings that had brightened the night only a moment before vanished into the darkness.

The ladies hurriedly closed the shutters and spoke of God. At that very moment, the chimes of midnight were again heard from below.